His Evening Out

By

Jerome K Jerome

British Library Cataloguing-in-Publication Data
A catalogue record for this book is available from the
British Library

Jerome K. Jerome

Jerome Klapka Jerome was born in Walsall, England in 1859. Both his parents died while he was in his early teens, and he was forced to quit school to support himself. Jerome worked for a number of years collecting coal along railway tracks, before trying his hand at acting, journalism, teaching and soliciting. At long last, in 1885, he had some success with *On the Stage – and Off,* a comic memoir of his experiences with an acting troupe. Jerome produced a number of essays over the following years, and married in 1888, spending the honeymoon in "a little boat" on the Thames.

In 1889, Jerome published his most successful and best-remembered work, *Three Men in a Boat.* Featuring himself and two of his friends encountering humorous situations while floating down the Thames in a small boat, the book was an instant success, and has never been out of print. In fact, its popularity was such that the number of registered Thames boats went up fifty percent in the year following its publication. With the financial security provided by *Three Men in a Boat,* Jerome was able to dedicate himself fully to writing, producing eleven more novels and a number of anthologies of short fiction.

In 1926, Jerome published his autobiography, *My Life and Times.* He died a year later, aged 68.

The evidence of the park-keeper, David Bristow, of Gilder Street, Camden Town, is as follows:

I was on duty in St. James's Park on Thursday evening, my sphere extending from the Mall to the northern shore of the ornamental water east of the suspension bridge. At five-and-twenty to seven I took up a position between the peninsula and the bridge to await my colleague. He ought to have relieved me at half-past six, but did not arrive until a few minutes before seven, owing, so he explained, to the breaking down of his motor-'bus--which may have been true or may not, as the saying is.

I had just come to a halt, when my attention was arrested by a lady. I am unable to explain why the presence of a lady in St. James's Park should have seemed in any way worthy of notice except that, for certain reasons, she reminded me of my first wife. I observed that she hesitated between one of the public seats and two vacant chairs standing by themselves a little farther to the east. Eventually she selected one of the chairs, and, having cleaned it with an evening paper--the birds in this portion of the Park being extremely prolific--sat down upon it. There was plenty of room upon the public seat close to it, except for some children who were playing touch; and in consequence of this I judged her to be a person of means.

I walked to a point from where I could command the southern approaches to the bridge, my colleague arriving sometimes by way of Birdcage Walk and sometimes by way of the Horse Guards Parade. Not seeing any signs of him in the direction of the bridge, I turned back. A little way past the chair where the lady was sitting I met Mr. Parable. I know Mr. Parable quite well by sight. He was wearing the usual grey suit and soft felt hat with which the pictures in the newspapers have made us all familiar. I judged that Mr. Parable had come from the Houses of Parliament, and the next morning my suspicions were confirmed by reading that he had been present at a tea-party given on the terrace by Mr. Will Crooks. Mr. Parable conveyed to me the suggestion of a man absorbed in thought, and not quite aware of what he was doing; but in this, of course, I may have been mistaken. He paused for a moment to look over the railings at the pelican. Mr. Parable said something to the pelican which I was not near enough to overhear; and then, still apparently in a state of abstraction, crossed the path and seated himself on the chair next to that occupied by the young lady.

From the tree against which I was standing I was able to watch the subsequent proceedings unobserved. The lady looked at Mr. Parable and then turned away and smiled to herself. It was a peculiar smile, and, again in some way I am unable to explain, reminded me of my first wife. It was not till the pelican put down his other leg and walked away that Mr. Parable, turning his gaze westward, became aware of the lady's presence.

From information that has subsequently come to my knowledge, I am prepared to believe that Mr. Parable, from the beginning, really thought the lady was a friend of his. What the lady thought is a matter for conjecture; I can only speak to the facts. Mr. Parable looked at the lady once or twice. Indeed, one might say with truth that he kept on doing it. The lady, it must be admitted, behaved for a while with extreme propriety; but after a time, as I felt must happen, their eyes met, and then it was I heard her say:

"Good evening, Mr. Parable."

She accompanied the words with the same peculiar smile to which I have already alluded. The exact words of Mr. Parable's reply I cannot remember. But it was to the effect that he had thought from the first that he had known her but had not been quite sure. It was at this point that, thinking I saw my colleague approaching, I went to meet him. I found I was mistaken, and slowly retraced my steps. I passed Mr. Parable and the lady. They were talking together with what I should describe as animation. I went as far as the southern extremity of the suspension bridge, and must have waited there quite ten minutes before returning eastward. It was while I was passing behind them on the grass, partially screened by the rhododendrons, that I heard Mr. Parable say to the lady:

"Why shouldn't we have it together?"

To which the lady replied:

"But what about Miss Clebb?"

I could not overhear what followed, owing to their sinking their voices. It seemed to be an argument. It ended with the young lady laughing and then rising. Mr. Parable also rose, and they walked off together. As they passed me I heard the lady say:

"I wonder if there's any place in London where you're not likely to be recognised."

Mr. Parable, who gave me the idea of being in a state of growing excitement, replied quite loudly:

"Oh, let 'em!"

I was following behind them when the lady suddenly stopped.

"I know!" she said. "The Popular Cafe."

The park-keeper said he was convinced he would know the lady again, having taken particular notice of her. She had brown eyes and was wearing a black hat supplemented with poppies.

* * *

Arthur Horton, waiter at the Popular Cafe, states as follows:

I know Mr. John Parable by sight. Have often heard him speak at public meetings. Am a bit of a Socialist myself. Remember his dining at the Popular Cafe on the evening of Thursday. Didn't recognise him immediately on his entrance for two reasons. One was his hat, and the other was his girl. I took it from him and hung it up. I mean, of course, the hat. It was a brand-new bowler, a trifle ikey about the brim. Have always associated him with a soft grey felt. But never with girls. Females, yes, to any extent. But this was the real article. You know what I mean--the sort of girl that you turn round to look after. It was she who selected the table in the corner behind the door. Been there before, I should say.

I should, in the ordinary course of business, have addressed Mr. Parable by name, such being our instructions in the case of customers known to us. But, putting the hat and the girl together, I decided not to. Mr. Parable was all for our three-and-six-penny table d'hote; he evidently not wanting to think. But the lady wouldn't hear of it.

"Remember Miss Clebb," she reminded him.

Of course, at the time I did not know what was meant. She ordered thin soup, a grilled sole, and cutlets au gratin. It certainly couldn't have been the dinner. With regard to the champagne, he would have his own way. I picked him out a dry '94, that you might have weaned a baby on. I suppose it was the whole thing combined.

It was after the sole that I heard Mr. Parable laugh. I could hardly credit my ears, but half-way through the cutlets he did it again.

There are two kinds of women. There is the woman who, the more she eats and drinks, the stodgier she gets, and the woman who lights up after it. I suggested a peche Melba between them, and when I returned with it, Mr. Parable was sitting with his elbows on the table gazing across at her with an expression that I can only describe as quite human. It was when I brought the coffee that he turned to me and asked:

"What's doing? Nothing stuffy," he added. "Is there an Exhibition anywhere--something in the open air?"

"You are forgetting Miss Clebb," the lady reminded him.

"For two pins," said Mr. Parable, "I would get up at the meeting and tell Miss Clebb what I really think about her."

I suggested the Earl's Court Exhibition, little thinking at the time what it was going to lead to; but the lady at first wouldn't hear of it, and the party at the next table calling for their bill (they had asked for it once or twice before, when I came to think of it), I had to go across to them.

When I got back the argument had just concluded, and the lady was holding up her finger.

"On condition that we leave at half-past nine, and that you go straight to Caxton Hall," she said.

"We'll see about it," said Mr. Parable, and offered me half a crown.

Tips being against the rules, I couldn't take it. Besides, one of the jumpers had his eye on me. I explained to him, jocosely, that I was doing it for a bet. He was surprised when I handed him his hat, but, the lady whispering to him, he remembered himself in time.

As they went out together I heard Mr. Parable say to the lady:

"It's funny what a shocking memory I have for names."

To which the lady replied:

"You'll think it funnier still to-morrow." And then she laughed.

Mr. Horton thought he would know the lady again. He puts down her age at about twenty-six, describing her--to use his own piquant expression--as "a bit of all right." She had brown eyes and a taking way with her.

* * *

Miss Ida Jenks, in charge of the Eastern Cigarette Kiosk at the Earl's Court Exhibition, gives the following particulars:

From where I generally stand I can easily command a view of the interior of the Victoria Hall; that is, of course, to say when the doors are open, as on a warm night is usually the case.

On the evening of Thursday, the twenty-seventh, it was fairly well occupied, but not to any great extent. One couple attracted my attention by reason of the gentleman's erratic steering. Had he been my partner I should have suggested a polka, the tango not being the sort of dance that can be picked up in an evening. What I mean to say is, that he struck me as being more willing than experienced. Some of the bumps she got would have made me cross; but we all have our fancies, and, so far as I could judge, they both appeared to be enjoying themselves. It was after the "Hitchy Koo" that they came outside.

The seat to the left of the door is popular by reason of its being partly screened by bushes, but by leaning forward a little it is quite possible for me to see what goes on there. They were the first couple out, having had a bad collision near the bandstand, so easily secured it. The gentleman was laughing.

There was something about him from the first that made me think I knew him, and when he took off his hat to wipe his head it came to me all of a sudden, he being the exact image of his effigy at Madame Tussaud's, which, by a curious coincidence, I happened to have visited with a friend that very afternoon. The lady was what some people would call good-looking, and others mightn't.

I was watching them, naturally a little interested. Mr. Parable, in helping the lady to adjust her cloak, drew her--it may have been by accident--towards him; and then it was that a florid gentleman with a short pipe in his mouth stepped forward and addressed the lady. He raised his hat and, remarking "Good evening," added that he hoped she was "having a pleasant time." His tone, I should explain, was sarcastic.

The young woman, whatever else may be said of her, struck me as behaving quite correctly. Replying to his salutation with a cold and distant bow, she rose, and, turning to Mr. Parable, observed that she thought it was perhaps time for them to be going.

The gentleman, who had taken his pipe from his mouth, said--again in a sarcastic tone--that he thought so too, and offered the lady his arm.

"I don't think we need trouble you," said Mr. Parable, and stepped between them.

To describe what followed I, being a lady, am hampered for words. I remember seeing Mr. Parable's hat go up into the air, and then the next moment the florid gentleman's head was lying on my counter smothered in cigarettes. I naturally screamed for the police, but the crowd was dead against me; and it was only after what I believe in technical language would be termed "the fourth round" that they appeared upon the scene.

The last I saw of Mr. Parable he was shaking a young constable who had lost his helmet, while three other policemen had hold of him from behind. The florid gentleman's hat I found on the floor of my kiosk and returned to him; but after a useless attempt to get it on his head, he disappeared with it in his hand. The lady was nowhere to be seen.

Miss Jenks thinks she would know her again. She was wearing a hat trimmed with black chiffon and a spray of poppies, and was slightly freckled.

* * *

Superintendent S. Wade, in answer to questions put to him by our representative, vouchsafed the following replies:

Yes. I was in charge at the Vine Street Police Station on the night of Thursday, the twenty-seventh.

No. I have no recollection of a charge of any description being preferred against any gentleman of the name of Parable.

Yes. A gentleman was brought in about ten o'clock charged with brawling at the Earl's Court Exhibition and assaulting a constable in the discharge of his duty.

The gentleman gave the name of Mr. Archibald Quincey, Harcourt Buildings, Temple.

No. The gentleman made no application respecting bail, electing to pass the night in the cells. A certain amount of discretion is permitted to us, and we made him as comfortable as possible.

Yes. A lady.

No. About a gentleman who had got himself into trouble at the Earl's Court Exhibition. She mentioned no name.

I showed her the charge sheet. She thanked me and went away.

That I cannot say. I can only tell you that at nine-fifteen on Friday morning bail was tendered, and, after inquiries, accepted in the person of Julius Addison Tupp, of the Sunnybrook Steam Laundry, Twickenham.

That is no business of ours.

The accused who, I had seen to it, had had a cup of tea and a little toast at seven-thirty, left in company with Mr. Tupp soon after ten.

Superintendent Wade admitted he had known cases where accused parties, to avoid unpleasantness, had stated their names to be other than their own, but declined to discuss the matter further.

Superintendent Wade, while expressing his regret that he had no more time to bestow upon our representative, thought it highly probable that he would know the lady again if he saw her.

Without professing to be a judge of such matters, Superintendent Wade thinks she might be described as a highly intelligent young woman, and of exceptionally prepossessing appearance.

* * *

From Mr. Julius Tupp, of the Sunnybrook Steam Laundry, Twickenham, upon whom our representative next called, we have been unable to obtain much assistance, Mr. Tupp replying to all questions put to him by the one formula, "Not talking."

Fortunately, our representative, on his way out through the drying ground, was able to obtain a brief interview with Mrs. Tupp.

Mrs. Tupp remembers admitting a young lady to the house on the morning of Friday, the twenty-eighth, when she opened the door to take in the milk. The lady, Mrs. Tupp remembers, spoke in a husky voice, the result, as the young lady explained with a pleasant laugh, of having passed the night wandering about Ham Common, she having been misdirected the previous evening by a fool of a railway porter, and not wishing to disturb the neighbourhood by waking people up at two o'clock in the morning, which, in Mrs. Tupp's opinion, was sensible of her.

Mrs. Tupp describes the young lady as of agreeable manners, but looking, naturally, a bit washed out. The lady asked for Mr. Tupp, explaining that a friend of his was in trouble, which did not in the least surprise Mrs. Tupp, she herself not holding with Socialists and such like. Mr. Tupp, on being informed, dressed hastily and went downstairs, and he and the young lady left the house together. Mr. Tupp, on being questioned as to the name of his friend, had called up that it was no one Mrs. Tupp would know, a Mr. Quince--it may have been Quincey.

Mrs. Tupp is aware that Mr. Parable is also a Socialist, and is acquainted with the saying about thieves hanging together. But has worked for Mr. Parable for years and has always found him a most satisfactory client; and, Mr. Tupp appearing at this point, our representative thanked Mrs. Tupp for her information and took his departure.

* * *

Mr. Horatius Condor, Junior, who consented to partake of luncheon in company with our representative at the Holborn Restaurant, was at first disinclined to be of much assistance, but eventually supplied our representative with the following information:

My relationship to Mr. Archibald Quincey, Harcourt Buildings, Temple, is perhaps a little difficult to define.

How he himself regards me I am never quite sure. There will be days together when we will be quite friendly like, and at other times he will be that offhanded and peremptory you might think I was his blooming office boy.

On Friday morning, the twenty-eighth, I didn't get to Harcourt Buildings at the usual time, knowing that Mr. Quincey would not be there himself, he having arranged to interview Mr. Parable for the Daily Chronicle at ten o'clock. I allowed him half an hour, to be quite safe, and he came in at a quarter past eleven.

He took no notice of me. For about ten minutes--it may have been less--he walked up and down the room, cursing and swearing and kicking the furniture about. He landed an occasional walnut table in the middle of my shins, upon which I took the opportunity of wishing him "Good morning," and he sort of woke up, as you might say.

"How did the interview go off?" I says. "Got anything interesting?"

"Yes," he says; "quite interesting. Oh, yes, decidedly interesting."

He was holding himself in, if you understand, speaking with horrible slowness and deliberation.

"D'you know where he was last night?" he asks me.

"Yes," I says; "Caxton Hall, wasn't it?--meeting to demand the release of Miss Clebb."

He leans across the table till his face was within a few inches of mine.

"Guess again," he says.

I wasn't doing any guessing. He had hurt me with the walnut table, and I was feeling a bit short-tempered.

"Oh! don't make a game of it," I says. "It's too early in the morning."

"At the Earl's Court Exhibition," he says; "dancing the tango with a lady that he picked up in St. James's Park."

"Well," I says, "why not? He don't often get much fun." I thought it best to treat it lightly.

He takes no notice of my observation.

"A rival comes upon the scene," he continues--"a fatheaded ass, according to my information--and they have a stand-up fight. He gets run in and spends the night in a Vine Street police cell."

I suppose I was grinning without knowing it.

"Funny, ain't it?" he says.

"Well," I says, "it has its humorous side, hasn't it? What'll he get?"

"I am not worrying about what HE is going to get," he answers back. "I am worrying about what _I_ am going to get."

I thought he had gone dotty.

"What's it got to do with you?" I says.

"If old Wotherspoon is in a good humour," he continues, "and the constable's head has gone down a bit between now and Wednesday, I may get off with forty shillings and a public reprimand.

"On the other hand," he goes on--he was working himself into a sort of fit--"if the constable's head goes on swelling, and old Wotherspoon's liver gets worse, I've got to be prepared for a month without the option. That is, if I am fool enough--"

He had left both the doors open, which in the daytime we generally do, our chambers being at the top. Miss Dorton--that's Mr. Parable's secretary--barges into the room. She didn't seem to notice me. She staggers to a chair and bursts into tears.

"He's gone," she says; "he's taken cook with him and gone."

"Gone!" says the guv'nor. "Where's he gone?"

"To Fingest," she says through her sobs--"to the cottage. Miss Bulstrode came in just after you had left," she says. "He wants to get away from everyone and have a few days' quiet. And then he is coming back, and he is going to do it himself."

"Do what?" says the guv'nor, irritable like.

"Fourteen days," she wails. "It'll kill him."

"But the case doesn't come on till Wednesday," says the guv'nor. "How do you know it's going to be fourteen days?"

"Miss Bulstrode," she says, "she's seen the magistrate. He says he always gives fourteen days in cases of unprovoked assault."

"But it wasn't unprovoked," says the guv'nor. "The other man began it by knocking off his hat. It was self-defence."

"She put that to him," she says, "and he agreed that that would alter his view of the case. But, you see," she continues, "we can't find the other man. He isn't likely to come forward of his own accord."

"The girl must know," says the guv'nor--"this girl he picks up in St. James's Park, and goes dancing with. The man must have been some friend of hers."

"But we can't find her either," she says. "He doesn't even know her name--he can't remember it."

"You will do it, won't you?" she says.

"Do what?" says the guv'nor again.

"The fourteen days," she says.

"But I thought you said he was going to do it himself?" he says.

"But he mustn't," she says. "Miss Bulstrode is coming round to see you. Think of it! Think of the headlines in the papers," she says. "Think of the Fabian Society. Think of the Suffrage cause. We mustn't let him."

"What about me?" says the guv'nor. "Doesn't anybody care for me?"

"You don't matter," she says. "Besides," she says, "with your influence you'll be able to keep it out of the papers. If it comes out that it was Mr. Parable, nothing on earth will be able to."

The guv'nor was almost as much excited by this time as she was.

"I'll see the Fabian Society and the Women's Vote and the Home for Lost Cats at Battersea, and all the rest of the blessed bag of tricks--"

I'd been thinking to myself, and had just worked it out.

"What's he want to take his cook down with him for?" I says.

"To cook for him," says the guv'nor. "What d'you generally want a cook for?"

"Rats!" I says. "Does he usually take his cook with him?"

"No," answered Miss Dorton. "Now I come to think of it, he has always hitherto put up with Mrs. Meadows."

"You will find the lady down at Fingest," I says, "sitting opposite him and enjoying a recherche dinner for two."

The guv'nor slaps me on the back, and lifts Miss Dorton out of her chair.

"You get on back," he says, "and telephone to Miss Bulstrode. I'll be round at half-past twelve."

Miss Dorton went out in a dazed sort of condition, and the guv'nor gives me a sovereign, and tells me I can have the rest of the day to myself.

Mr. Condor, Junior, considers that what happened subsequently goes to prove that he was right more than it proves that he was wrong.

Mr. Condor, Junior, also promised to send us a photograph of himself for reproduction, but, unfortunately, up to the time of going to press it had not arrived.

* * *

From Mrs. Meadows, widow of the late Corporal John Meadows, V.C., Turberville, Bucks, the following further particulars were obtained by our local representative:

I have done for Mr. Parable now for some years past, my cottage being only a mile off, which makes it easy for me to look after him.

Mr. Parable likes the place to be always ready so that he can drop in when he chooses, he sometimes giving me warning and sometimes not. It was about the end of last month--on a Friday, if I remember rightly--that he suddenly turned up.

As a rule, he walks from Henley station, but on this occasion he arrived in a fly, he having a young woman with him, and she having a bag--his cook, as he explained to me. As a rule, I do everything for Mr. Parable, sleeping in the cottage when he is there; but to tell the truth, I was glad to see her. I never was much of a cook myself, as my poor dead husband has remarked on more than one occasion, and I don't pretend to be. Mr. Parable added, apologetic like, that he had been suffering lately from indigestion.

"I am only too pleased to see her," I says. "There are the two beds in my room, and we shan't quarrel." She was quite a sensible young woman, as I had judged from the first look at her, though suffering at the time from a cold. She hires a bicycle from Emma Tidd, who only uses it on a Sunday, and, taking a market basket, off she starts for Henley, Mr. Parable saying he would go with her to show her the way.

They were gone a goodish time, which, seeing it's eight miles, didn't so much surprise me; and when they got back we all three had dinner together, Mr. Parable arguing that it made for what he called "labour saving." Afterwards I cleared away, leaving them talking together; and later on they had a walk round the garden, it being a moonlight night, but a bit too cold for my fancy.

In the morning I had a chat with her before he was down. She seemed a bit worried.

"I hope people won't get talking," she says. "He would insist on my coming."

"Well," I says, "surely a gent can bring his cook along with him to cook for him. And as for people talking, what I always say is, one may just as well give them something to talk about and save them the trouble of making it up."

"If only I was a plain, middle-aged woman," she says, "it would be all right."

"Perhaps you will be, all in good time," I says, but, of course, I could see what she was driving at. A nice, clean, pleasant-faced young woman she was, and not of the ordinary class. "Meanwhile," I says, "if you don't mind taking a bit of motherly advice, you might remember that your place is the kitchen, and his the parlour. He's a dear good man, I know, but human nature is human nature, and it's no good pretending it isn't."

She and I had our breakfast together before he was up, so that when he came down he had to have his alone, but afterwards she comes into the kitchen and closes the door.

"He wants to show me the way to High Wycombe," she says. "He will have it there are better shops at Wycombe. What ought I to do?"

My experience is that advising folks to do what they don't want to do isn't the way to do it.

"What d'you think yourself?" I asked her.

"I feel like going with him," she says, "and making the most of every mile."

And then she began to cry.

"What's the harm!" she says. "I have heard him from a dozen platforms ridiculing class distinctions. Besides," she says, "my people have been farmers for generations. What was Miss Bulstrode's father but a grocer? He ran a hundred shops instead of one. What difference does that make?"

"When did it all begin?" I says. "When did he first take notice of you like?"

"The day before yesterday," she answers. "He had never seen me before," she says. "I was just 'Cook'-- something in a cap and apron that he passed occasionally on the stairs. On Thursday he saw me in my best clothes, and fell in love with me. He doesn't know it himself, poor dear, not yet, but that's what he's done."

Well, I couldn't contradict her, not after the way I had seen him looking at her across the table.

"What are your feelings towards him," I says, "to be quite honest? He's rather a good catch for a young person in your position."

"That's my trouble," she says. "I can't help thinking of that. And then to be 'Mrs. John Parable'! That's enough to turn a woman's head."

"He'd be a bit difficult to live with," I says.

"Geniuses always are," she says; "it's easy enough if you just think of them as children. He'd be a bit fractious at times, that's all. Underneath, he's just the kindest, dearest--"

"Oh, you take your basket and go to High Wycombe," I says. "He might do worse."

I wasn't expecting them back soon, and they didn't come back soon. In the afternoon a motor stops at the gate, and out of it steps Miss Bulstrode, Miss Dorton--that's the young lady that writes for him--and Mr. Quincey. I told them I couldn't say when he'd be back, and they said it didn't matter, they just happening to be passing.

"Did anybody call on him yesterday?" asks Miss Bulstrode, careless like--"a lady?"

"No," I says; "you are the first as yet."

"He's brought his cook down with him, hasn't he?" says Mr. Quincey.

"Yes," I says, "and a very good cook too," which was the truth.

"I'd like just to speak a few words with her," says Miss Bulstrode.

"Sorry, m'am," I says, "but she's out at present; she's gone to Wycombe."

"Gone to Wycombe!" they all says together.

"To market," I says. "It's a little farther, but, of course, it stands to reason the shops there are better."

They looked at one another.

"That settles it," says Mr. Quincey. "Delicacies worthy to be set before her not available nearer than Wycombe, but must be had. There's going to be a pleasant little dinner here to-night."

"The hussy!" says Miss Bulstrode, under her breath.

They whispered together for a moment, then they turns to me.

"Good afternoon, Mrs. Meadows," says Mr. Quincey. "You needn't say we called. He wanted to be alone, and it might vex him."

I said I wouldn't, and I didn't. They climbed back into the motor and went off.

Before dinner I had call to go into the woodshed. I heard a scuttling as I opened the door. If I am not mistaken, Miss Dorton was hiding in the corner where we keep the coke. I didn't see any good in making a fuss, so I left her there. When I got back to the kitchen, cook asked me if we'd got any parsley.

"You'll find a bit in the front," I says, "to the left of the gate," and she went out. She came back looking scared.

"Anybody keep goats round here?" she asked me.

"Not that I know of, nearer than Ibstone Common," I says.

"I could have sworn I saw a goat's face looking at me out of the gooseberry bushes while I was picking the parsley," she says. "It had a beard."

"It's the half light," I says. "One can imagine anything."

"I do hope I'm not getting nervy," she says.

I thought I'd have another look round, and made the excuse that I wanted a pail of water. I was stooping over the well, which is just under the mulberry tree, when something fell close to me and lodged upon the bricks. It was a hairpin. I fixed the cover carefully upon the well in case of accident, and when I got in I went round myself and was careful to see that all the curtains were drawn.

Just before we three sat down to dinner again I took cook aside.

"I shouldn't go for any stroll in the garden to-night," I says. "People from the village may be about, and we don't want them gossiping." And she thanked me.

Next night they were there again. I thought I wouldn't spoil the dinner, but mention it afterwards. I saw to it again that the curtains were drawn, and slipped the catch of both the doors. And just as well that I did.

I had always heard that Mr. Parable was an amusing speaker, but on previous visits had not myself noticed it. But this time he seemed ten years younger than I had ever known him before; and during dinner, while we were talking and laughing quite merry like, I had the feeling more than once that people were meandering about outside. I had just finished clearing away, and cook was making the coffee, when there came a knock at the door.

"Who's that?" says Mr. Parable. "I am not at home to anyone."

"I'll see," I says. And on my way I slipped into the kitchen.

"Coffee for one, cook," I says, and she understood. Her cap and apron were hanging behind the door. I flung them across to her, and she caught them; and then I opened the front door.

They pushed past me without speaking, and went straight into the parlour. And they didn't waste many words on him either.

"Where is she?" asked Miss Bulstrode.

"Where's who?" says Mr. Parable.

"Don't lie about it," said Miss Bulstrode, making no effort to control herself. "The hussy you've been dining with?"

"Do you mean Mrs. Meadows?" says Mr. Parable.

I thought she was going to shake him.

"Where have you hidden her?" she says.

It was at that moment cook entered with the coffee.

If they had taken the trouble to look at her they might have had an idea. The tray was trembling in her hands, and in her haste and excitement she had put on her cap the wrong way round. But she kept control of her voice, and asked if she should bring some more coffee.

"Ah, yes! You'd all like some coffee, wouldn't you?" says Mr. Parable. Miss Bulstrode did not reply, but Mr. Quincey said he was cold and would like it. It was a nasty night, with a thin rain.

"Thank you, sir," says cook, and we went out together.

Cottages are only cottages, and if people in the parlour persist in talking loudly, people in the kitchen can't very well help overhearing.

There was a good deal of talk about "fourteen days," which Mr. Parable said he was going to do himself, and which Miss Dorton said he mustn't, because, if he did, it would be a victory for the enemies of humanity. Mr. Parable said something about "humanity," which I didn't rightly hear, but, whatever it was, it started Miss Dorton crying; and Miss Bulstrode called Mr. Parable a "blind Samson," who had had his hair cut by a designing minx who had been hired to do it.

It was all French to me, but cook was drinking in every word, and when she returned from taking them in their coffee she made no bones about it, but took up her place at the door with her ear to the keyhole.

It was Mr. Quincey who got them all quiet, and then he began to explain things. It seemed that if they could only find a certain gentleman and persuade him to come forward and acknowledge that he began a row, that then all would be well. Mr. Quincey would be fined forty shillings, and Mr. Parable's name would never appear. Failing that, Mr. Parable, according to Mr. Quincey, could do his fourteen days himself.

"I've told you once," says Mr. Parable, "and I tell you again, that I don't know the man's name, and can't give it you."

"We are not asking you to," says Mr. Quincey. "You give us the name of your tango partner, and we'll do the rest."

I could see cook's face; I had got a bit interested myself, and we were both close to the door. She hardly seemed to be breathing.

"I am sorry," says Mr. Parable, speaking very deliberate-like, "but I am not going to have her name dragged into this business."

"It wouldn't be," says Mr. Quincey. "All we want to get out of her is the name and address of the gentleman who was so anxious to see her home."

"Who was he?" says Miss Bulstrode. "Her husband?"

"No," says Mr. Parable; "he wasn't."

"Then who was he?" says Miss Bulstrode. "He must have been something to her--fiance?"

"I am going to do the fourteen days myself," says Mr. Parable. "I shall come out all the fresher after a fortnight's complete rest and change."

Cook leaves the door with a smile on her face that made her look quite beautiful, and, taking some paper from the dresser drawer, began to write a letter.

They went on talking in the other room for another ten minutes, and then Mr. Parable lets them out himself, and goes a little way with them. When he came back we could hear him walking up and down the other room.

She had written and stamped the envelope; it was lying on the table.

"'Joseph Onions, Esq.,'" I says, reading the address. "'Auctioneer and House Agent, Broadway, Hammersmith.' Is that the young man?"

"That is the young man," she says, folding her letter and putting it in the envelope.

"And was he your fiance?" I asked.

"No," she says. "But he will be if he does what I'm telling him to do."

"And what about Mr. Parable?" I says.

"A little joke that will amuse him later on," she says, slipping a cloak on her shoulders. "How once he nearly married his cook."

"I shan't be a minute," she says. And, with the letter in her hand, she slips out.

Mrs. Meadows, we understand, has expressed indignation at our publication of this interview, she being under the impression that she was simply having a friendly gossip with a neighbour. Our representative, however, is sure he explained to Mrs. Meadows that his visit was official; and, in any case, our duty to the public must be held to exonerate us from all blame in the matter.

* * *

Mr. Joseph Onions, of the Broadway, Hammersmith, auctioneer and house agent, expressed himself to our representative as most surprised at the turn that events had subsequently taken. The letter that Mr. Onions received from Miss Comfort Price was explicit and definite. It was to the effect that if he would call upon a certain Mr. Quincey, of Harcourt Buildings, Temple, and acknowledge that it was he who began the row at the Earl's Court Exhibition on the evening of the twenty-seventh, that then the engagement between himself and Miss Price, hitherto unacknowledged by the lady, might be regarded as a fact.

Mr. Onions, who describes himself as essentially a business man, decided before complying with Miss Price's request to take a few preliminary steps. As the result of judiciously conducted inquiries, first at the Vine Street Police Station, and secondly at Twickenham, Mr. Onions arrived later in the day at Mr. Quincey's chambers, with, to use his own expression, all the cards in his hand. It was Mr. Quincey who, professing himself unable to comply with Mr. Onion's suggestion, arranged the interview with Miss Bulstrode. And it was Miss Bulstrode herself who, on condition that Mr. Onions added to the undertaking the further condition that he would marry Miss Price before the end of the month, offered to make it two hundred. It was in their joint interest--Mr. Onions regarding himself and Miss Price as now one--that Mr. Onions suggested her making it three, using such arguments as, under the circumstances, naturally occurred to him--as, for example, the damage caused to the lady's reputation by the whole proceedings, culminating in a night spent by the lady, according to her own account, on Ham Common. That the price demanded was reasonable Mr. Onions considers as proved by Miss Bulstrode's eventual acceptance of his terms. That, having got out of him all that he wanted, Mr. Quincey should have "considered it his duty" to communicate the entire details of the transaction to Miss Price, through the medium of Mr. Andrews, thinking it "as well she should know the character of the man she proposed to marry," Mr. Onions considers a gross breach of etiquette as between gentlemen; and having regard to Miss Price's after behaviour, Mr. Onions can only say that she is not the girl he took her for.

Mr. Aaron Andrews, on whom our representative called, was desirous at first of not being drawn into the matter; but on our representative explaining to him that our only desire was to contradict false rumours likely to be harmful to Mr. Parable's reputation, Mr. Andrews saw the necessity of putting our representative in possession of the truth.

She came back on Tuesday afternoon, explained Mr. Andrews, and I had a talk with her.

"It is all right, Mr. Andrews," she told me; "they've been in communication with my young man, and Miss Bulstrode has seen the magistrate privately. The case will be dismissed with a fine of forty shillings, and Mr. Quincey has arranged to keep it out of the papers."

"Well, all's well that ends well," I answered; "but it might have been better, my girl, if you had mentioned that young man of yours a bit earlier."

"I did not know it was of any importance," she explained. "Mr. Parable told me nothing. If it hadn't been for chance, I should never have known what was happening."

I had always liked the young woman. Mr. Quincey had suggested my waiting till after Wednesday. But there seemed to me no particular object in delay.

"Are you fond of him?" I asked her.

"Yes," she answered. "I am fonder than--" And then she stopped herself suddenly and flared scarlet. "Who are you talking about?" she demanded.

"This young man of yours," I said. "Mr.--What's his name--Onions?"

"Oh, that?" she answered. "Oh, yes; he's all right."

"And if he wasn't?" I said, and she looked at me hard.

"I told him," she said, "that if he would do what I asked him to do, I'd marry him. And he seems to have done it."

"There are ways of doing everything," I said; and, seeing it wasn't going to break her heart, I told her just the plain facts. She listened without a word, and when I had finished she put her arms round my neck and kissed me. I am old enough to be her grandfather, but twenty years ago it might have upset me.

"I think I shall be able to save Miss Bulstrode that three hundred pounds," she laughed, and ran upstairs and changed her things. When later I looked into the kitchen she was humming.

Mr. John came up by the car, and I could see he was in one of his moods.

"Pack me some things for a walking tour," he said. "Don't forget the knapsack. I am going to Scotland by the eight-thirty."

"Will you be away long?" I asked him.

"It depends upon how long it takes me," he answered. "When I come back I am going to be married."

"Who is the lady?" I asked, though, of course, I knew.

"Miss Bulstrode," he said.

"Well," I said, "she--"

"That will do," he said; "I have had all that from the three of them for the last two days. She is a Socialist, and a Suffragist, and all the rest of it, and my ideal helpmate. She is well off, and that will enable me to devote all my time to putting the world to rights without bothering about anything else. Our home will be the nursery of advanced ideas. We shall share together the joys and delights of the public platform. What more can any man want?"

"You will want your dinner early," I said, "if you are going by the eight-thirty. I had better tell cook--"

He interrupted me again.

"You can tell cook to go to the devil," he said.

I naturally stared at him.

"She is going to marry a beastly little rotter of a rent collector that she doesn't care a damn for," he went on.

I could not understand why he seemed so mad about it.

"I don't see, in any case, what it's got to do with you," I said, "but, as a matter of fact, she isn't."

"Isn't what?" he said, stopping short and turning on me.

"Isn't going to marry him," I answered.

"Why not?" he demanded.

"Better ask her," I suggested.

I didn't know at the time that it was a silly thing to say, and I am not sure that I should not have said it if I had. When he is in one of his moods I always seem to get into one of mine. I have looked after Mr. John ever since he was a baby, so that we do not either of us treat the other quite as perhaps we ought to.

"Tell cook I want her," he said.

"She is just in the middle--" I began.

"I don't care where she is," he said. He seemed determined never to let me finish a sentence. "Send her up here."

She was in the kitchen by herself.

"He wants to see you at once," I said.

"Who does?" she asked.

"Mr. John," I said.

"What's he want to see me for?" she asked.

"How do I know?" I answered.

"But you do," she said. She always had an obstinate twist in her, and, feeling it would save time, I told her what had happened.

"Well," I said, "aren't you going?"

She was standing stock still staring at the pastry she was making. She turned to me, and there was a curious smile about her lips.

"Do you know what you ought to be wearing?" she said. "Wings, and a little bow and arrow."

She didn't even think to wipe her hands, but went straight upstairs. It was about half an hour later when the bell rang. Mr. John was standing by the window.

"Is that bag ready?" he said.

"It will be," I said.

I went out into the hall and returned with the clothes brush.

"What are you going to do?" he said.

"Perhaps you don't know it," I said, "but you are all over flour."

"Cook's going with me to Scotland," he said.

I have looked after Mr. John ever since he was a boy. He was forty-two last birthday, but when I shook hands with him through the cab window I could have sworn he was twenty-five again.

-THE END-